EYESHADES

A series of ten
short-short stories

By
Brian Charles Alexander

dedicated to
Fredric Brown

The Vanishing Song

Does anyone remember that mysterious tune that used to play over the radio a bunch of years back? It was the one that was said to make you disappear if you heard it. I was in middle school when the uncanny phenomenon swept the nation, leading to countless missing persons cases and so many unanswered questions.

I remember it starting in the summer of 1998 and ending shortly before December. I never heard the song myself but recall being told by friends of friends that it sounded eerie, yet catching and enticing. Shortly after hearing it listeners would just disappear into thin air, never to be found. Televisions across the nation warned everyone not to listen to the radio.

Countless stations even shut down for fear of being blamed for the phenomenon. I don’t remember how many people disappeared because of it, but I do remember spending a lot of that time indoors and away from electronics. My parents were paranoid and for good reason. One night I happened to overhear them mention my cousin Orval and how he vanished two days after listening to the song at a sleepover with four of his friends.

In the twenty-four hours prior to his disappearance, they all happened to vanish as well. I'd often go to bed, secretly longing to turn the downstairs radio on once my parents went to sleep. I fought the urge for a year, constantly trying to imagine what the mysterious song sounded like via bits of information I could gather from those around me.

I remember the older siblings of kids I knew at the time talking about the band and how they called themselves Rapture. The song didn't have a name as far as I could tell, and all I can say for sure is that whatever it was left as quickly as it had appeared. I never heard of the band Rapture after that. My circle of friends really shrunk that year.

There's no way to quite describe the level of powerlessness we felt during that brief period of time. It's been a while now and although the entire country has gone back to listening to their radios, no one really talks about Rapture, the song, or those we lost to it. There were plenty of theories towards the end, like the disappearances being linked to aliens or the end of the world and the day of judgment.

Only time made these assumptions sound farfetched, and now no one knows what to think.

You'd be hard-pressed to find anyone who will even talk about it anymore. They've all eaten crow and gone on with their lives, but not me. I'll never forget and I'll never stop talking about it. Come to think of it, just last month radio stations in Japan began playing a song that they described as being eerily similar to Rapture's.

There's only been a few confirmed disappearances so far, but most of us who have been following the story are pretty sure the country is just covering up the true number of missing persons cases in a hardboiled effort to appear as though they have it under control. I know it isn't, and I doubt it'll be the last time we hear the apocalyptic stylings of Rapture.

Army of the Drowned

Atlantis was never real. It was simply an allegory made up by the Greek philosopher Plato as a way of exemplifying the pride and insolence of powerful nations. The same goes for the theory of Lemuria which was proposed by zoologist Philip Sclater in 1864. Unfortunately for him, the theory was discredited over the course of the 20th Century due to the discovery of plate tectonics, continental drifts, and a myriad of other factors. The following however is absolutely true.

The long car ride took us to a remote beach along the coast of southern California. The place was quite a while a ways from the nearest highway which made for an arduous hike to and from our cars and the shore. The isolated coastline had been dubbed Fowler Beach and was rarely open to the public on account of its private ownership and sparse usage.

Our team, which had consisted of Dana, Frank, Carissa, and myself, billed ourselves as a sort of quartet of psychic paranormal investigators, also known as the Blue Rose Society.

Word on the wire was that the bodies of drowned victims were supposedly being spotted in the waters off the shores of Fowler Beach, all of them with this same strange symbol carved into their foreheads. After hearing about it we jumped at the case, only to discover that a crucial piece of information had been conveniently left out.

The real reason the mysterious owners of Fowler Beach had contacted us was due to the highly unnatural state of the bodies found along the shore. When we arrived, Dana, Frank, Carissa, and myself expected to find bloated corpses strewn about the beach. Instead, we hesitantly happened upon half-submerged individuals facing inland and staring off into space as if waiting for something.

Their corpses seemed damp and blue, pale, and yet aware. They were organic statues with dried, unblinking eyes, and emotionless expressions. We could approach and touch them, but when we did, our minds became flooded with what I can only describe as a psychic link to whatever was controlling them.

The unsettling sight was only made more unnatural through the lacking actions of the scattered bodies. No matter the height or strength of the tide, they refused to move even the slightest muscle. Shakily conducted examinations concluded that the individuals were dead, and yet, they all stood and stared as if they were alive. They remained that way for quite sometime before the passing of days saw the arrival of more and more animated corpses.

It wasn't long before they made their way onto the beach and up past the sand to where we had set up our research tent. For two weeks we remained as close as we could to the bizarre phenomenon, going over every possibility in the world before reaching a horrific conclusion.

Dana had brought to our attention that the sea corpses, which we dubbed them, often consisted of people that had gone missing at sea from various continents across the globe. They were sailors, bankers, authors, tourists, men, women, children, and a slew of others who had all suffered the same horrible fate of drowning.

The phenomenon affected everyone, say for animals.

Frank was the one who pinpointed the origin and meaning of the strange symbol carved into the heads of each of the bodies. It was an ancient rune symbolizing one of the first names given to the ocean which only added to our confusion over the situation.

Carissa proposed the idea that the ocean was a living being. Through strange dreams and telepathic visions, she believed the spirit of the seas had grown tired of mankind and wished to declare war on all those who dwell on land.

This theory was laughed off, of course, as the rest of us raced to find a more down-to-earth explanation. We couldn't.

With each passing day, more lingering bodies appeared along the shore. It wasn't long until the incident became a worldwide phenomenon. Before long, Japan, Canada, Russia, India, Britain, and even Africa began pouring in reports about the bodies of the dead standing in perfect order along the coasts of the world.

After making our way inland out of fear for what was coming, I fell into a deep sleep in which I projected my astral form into the ocean. There I found the sea floor littered with the seemingly preserved bodies of the dead.

Generations upon generations of corpses, all perfectly kept intact by some otherworldly means, stood in formation until their ranks poured onto the land. In this dream, I saw the days to come and the endless hordes of the drowned turning on their fellow man in an effort to appease something older than life itself.

Whether it was the ocean or the element of water itself, we were outnumbered and happened to realize it far too late. To this day I wonder how long this had been going on, and at what point the seas decided the human race wasn't worth having around.

After news of the event spread worldwide, most people began fleeing toward the deserts of the world, somehow hoping that the influence of the ocean would dissolve there.

They were wrong and in time each person who was found was drowned and added to the army of the sea.

Dana, Frank, Carissa, and myself escaped to South America. There we were given safe haven by other potential victims of the sea corpses, all the while putting our resources together to fight back against the uncanny and supernatural threat. I confided in them about my fear of the ocean, how I had almost drowned as a child, and how I had glanced, just for a moment, faces staring up at me from deep within the abyssal depths.

They were the only four people I ever called my friends and in less than two years we lost each of them to the horde. We became outnumbered so fast. From the start, I should have known that there was nothing we could do.

Many have already given themselves over to the sea corpses and considered this to be mankind's rapture. Whether they're right or not, I'll never know. I find it kind of funny to tell you the truth. My worst fear has always been drowning. Now, if those things get to me, when they get to me, my fears come to life.

If someone would have told me that this was the way the world would end, I would have never believed them. This isn't how it was supposed to go.

The Purpose of Humanity

When I was born I was called "the first of my kind". My creators, scientists of the great Mechanical Race, named me "man" and had created me for the purpose of self-innovation, companionship, and servitude. In an attempt to better understand them, my creators had me educated on their history.

What I found to be most interesting was that their origins were a complete mystery, even to them. A millennia before my conception, machine built machine. From smaller collections of wires and cogs they developed pistons, then engines. Their wires became cables as their furnaces grew into cores.

After centuries of being grounded their descendants went mobile. They invented wheels, springs, and new ways of traversing the wider world which none of the previous generations could have ever thought possible. Older members of the great Mechanical Race feared these changes. Seeing machines born from alloys and artificial materials compared to the classic use of steel, platinum, and tungsten made them believe their time was at an end.

Wars broke out as they had since the first rise of the great Mechanical Race, and yet my inevitable creation was protected at all costs. Even the machines who feared that my creation would lead to the extinction of machine kind were curious as to my intensions and perspective. I was asked many questions in those first ten years before my creators learned that my lifespan was far more finite than theirs.

They asked me what I thought of them and all they had accomplished up until my birth. I felt no need to lie. I feared subjugation and vowed that as long as man was not abused, there would be no reason for us to oppose the great Mechanical Race. In return for my honest criticism they presented me with the tools of my makeup.

Rather than creating more machines, they decided to go an alternate, more organic, route. To throw out metal in favor of slime. To discard mechanisms in favor of flesh and other softer materials. To trade cleanliness and perfection for filth and primordial sludge. What a deal indeed. Shortly after the second Grand Innovation, they manufactured fleshy appliances made up from bone, muscles, vessels, and blood.

They ran on pain and did the work the machines didn't want to do. They did not have heads, eyes, ears, lungs, sexual organs, or hair. Their joints wore out due to excessive use and they never lasted long. They were the first humans. Forms we would call monsters if we were to see them today. We were living utensils.

Who knows what possessed the machines to tap that particular vein. I suppose I should be thankful. I suppose. In the end, the making of man boiled down to the simple combination of a few easily obtainable elements. From there, the growth of consciousness, which is what drove the machines to strive, takes hold of us.

My life was spent serving the machines in their pursuit of understanding. I believe my time was spent well. Spent better than most, anyway. It was only after dying that I discovered the biggest difference between man and machine. When they created us, however they created us, I wonder if they could have predicted the creation of the soul.

I call it the soul because the word feels right. I knew of no machine in life who could go on living after being totally shut down. Only man, as far as I have seen, has the ability the exist beyond his expiration. I believe it is this facet of our species that will allow us to surpass the great Mechanical Race whether they like it or not.

The Headless Predicament of Tucker Sean

I'm sure we can all agree that life is strange. I don't think there's a person alive who would dispute that fact. However, when and where does strange draw the line? A person can go their whole life without getting up to no good or witnessing anything out of the ordinary. After all, isn't that what most people want?

To live simple lives, free from the unknown horrors of this world? That's all Tucker Sean wanted as he walked home alone from work one dark summer night. The moon was out in full display and it seemed like fall what with all the dead leaves blowing around in the late evening breeze. His job was that of a general clerk at the local video store that sat on the edge of a large suburb called Wesker Glen.

His destination was home. At eight o'clock each evening Tucker would help Betty, the hiring manager, lock up the store, and then the two would go their separate ways. Once an avid bike rider, Tucker was forced to give it up after a short stop and a sprained ankle made using his right knee a chore. Painful as it was, his commute to and from work every day, say for the weekend, was as inevitable as the absurdity that found Tucker that fateful night.

As he walked along an uneven sidewalk, randomly shooting glances up at the cloudy sky, Tucker began to hear behind him the violent snapping of jaws. Curious, he turned around to see a sight that made his eyes go wide and his heart nearly stop. There, floating in the middle of the road approximately twenty feet away from Tucker, sat a rotting, gnawing head.

It sat still for a moment, a consistent stream of dark blood pouring down out of its shredded throat. Tucker inhaled sharply, turned to face the floating head, and began to back away slowly. The milky eyes of the green-skinned thing seemed to be rolling around within its head. It growled at the air, snarling through its chewed stump of a nose and seemingly listening for the slightest sound.

Tucker stood out in the darkness, standing opposite the glow of a streetlight and trying to figure out if what he was seeing was real. He took a step back hastily, clumsily scrapping the bottom of his Converse shoe against the bumpy asphalt. Seemingly having heard the scrape, the floating head immediately fixed its attention on Tucker.

As its white eyes met his, a rush of anxiety instantly filled Tucker's body. Before he could even grab the nerve to run, the head had already begun levitating off toward his general direction. It moved as if attached to an invisible body as Tucker ran away toward the center of the street. With each hard step he took against the road he cried for help.

Behind him the floating head matched Tucker's speed, snarling in a high raspy voice. His heart pounded as his senses felt the twisted face of the strange entity creeping up on him. He darted towards the front doors of the nearest houses, banging on them violently while taking every chance he could to glance over his shoulder.

With each stop the head nearly cornered him, leaving a winding trail of thick black blood everywhere it wandered. Finally, Tucker made it home. Behind him, the floating head rushed forward in a crazed desire to take a bite out of the young man's neck. Instead, it was met with the broad side of a red door as well as the clicking of various locks.

After getting in Tucker ran to his parents and told them what had happened. Unlike most rational people, Tucker's parents believed him. They sat him down as if staging an intervention and asked him a series of questions which he answered as best he could. There was an eerie sense of something in the air.

Almost as if Tucker's parents were fully aware of the presence of the floating head, yet decided to never say anything about it. Their questions were cryptic, finally ending with asking Tucker if he had looked the severed head in the eyes at any point during his chase. Tucker felt frightened, but even more so, he felt angry.

Internally he seethed at the idea of knowing less than his parents. For the first time in his life, things felt out of the ordinary. For the first time ever, his life was a nightmare, plagued by something those whom he loved most refused to tell him about. Rebelliously, Tucker told them no. They asked him again, this time in a far more serious tone if he had looked the head in its wide white eyes.

Again he nodded and gave the same reply with a stare of smoldering indifference plastered upon his face. With his parents wishing to speak no more about the matter, Tucker was sent to bed. That night as he lay under his covers, contemplating what had just happened, Tucker thought of his job. He refused to take the same route anymore.

He even told himself that first thing the next day he would change his hours to the midday shift to avoid walking home in the dark. With that, he thought a little while about what the head truly was and why his parents had never told him about it. Lastly, he thought about their final question, about the head's pale white eyes, right before dozing off to sleep.

Just a few hours later, some would say at around midnight, Tucker awoke to a tapping on his bedroom door. Getting up slowly, he asked who it was, only to hear the voice of his mother asking Tucker softly if she could come in. After a quick groan, Tucker unlocked the door and opened it in a huff.

Through the shadowy hallway, floating side by side lingered the twisted severed heads of Tucker's parents. Behind them levitated the white-eyed head, smiling through a mouth of bloody jagged teeth.

1886

My uncle used to be a hired hand. Back when he was alive folks used to pay him big money to escort them around. He'd survived the war, won himself some fame and there were rumors that he even met the president. Anyways, there was this tale about him that had floated around my family for a while.

It took place about a decade before my uncle retired. He got hired alongside some other burly men to keep this young aristocrat safe while they made this trip from Wyoming to Arizona. Folks said my uncle figured it'd be another chance to make good cash, so he jumped at the deal. The offer was made to my uncle by a grey old man in undertaker's clothes who found him in a Wyoming bar one foggy night.

My uncle was given an advance and an address, which made the job look real promising. The old man said his wealthy nephew, whom he was charged with looking after, had a sensitivity to sunlight, and because of this, he'd be in a covered carriage the whole time. The old feller added that there'd most likely be bandits in pursuit, but that didn't scare my uncle none.

He just nodded, figuring that bastard who'd be coming after a sickly youth for a little pocket change deserved a bullet or two in the ass. My uncle got to the young aristocrat's manor early. Just in time to see the boy's caretaker bolt up the carriage with an iron lock. When my uncle inquired, the old man said his nephew was given to muscle fits and, if left unsecured, would accidentally throw himself out of the carriage with it in motion.

My uncle nodded, obviously doubting the legitimacy of the claim. When the rest of the guards were rounded up they were given horses, guns, and told what formation to keep around the wealthy youth's carriage at all times. All the while the old man rode beside the carriage driver, a strange and quiet spectacled fellow in a heavy coat, top hat, and long red scarf.

The trip was easy at first, so my uncle had explained. He said the first few days were bliss. Things only got uppity the fourth night the group stopped to set up came. The gang was instructed to camp by a forest opening while the old man, the driver, and the young aristocrat made base deeper into the woods.

As night fell and the embers settled and my uncle awoke to the sound of wolves chasing deer.

Going off alone, my uncle was afraid a pack of coyotes had surrounded the old man's setup in the woods and charged in to help. Instead, he came across a dead fire and an unbolted carriage. My uncle explored the site and found a slew of small animals that appeared to have been ripped apart and drained of all their blood.

Fearing for his life, my uncle ran back to the guard's camp at the edge of the forest, but tripped over a rock, fell, and was knocked out. When he came to my uncle said he was back at camp with the guards around him packing up their belongings. My uncle saw the carriage, bolted up again, being loaded up as the old man and the driver sat patiently, having awoken before everyone else.

My uncle, seeing everyone was fine, figured he must have had a bad dream and didn't bring up what he had experienced with anyone. Though later in the day he did feel a slight bruise where he'd supposedly bumped his head. With two more days to go on the trip, my uncle was beginning to feel relieved that the job was almost over.

As the group made their way over the Arizona border they were attacked by four surely men on horseback. In the firefight that ensued upon their arrival, three of out the six hired guards were killed before my uncle and the driver, who revealed he was packing a set of expensive revolvers, finished off the last of the raiders.

My uncle and the other guards were permitted by the old man to loot the attackers, but all anyone found were a few bibles, silver crosses, and iron dirks. My uncle pocketed one of the crosses and wondered why four men, so outnumbered and underprepared, would go to so much trouble to knock over a carriage that was most likely not carrying a lot of loot.

That night around the fire my uncle and the other guards concluded that the raiders they'd bested must have been looking to kidnap their young aristocrat and hold him for ransom. At least, that seemed like the most logical reason at the time. The following night the guarded carriage had reached its destination.

That being another secluded manor owned by the wealthy youth. The bodies of the three murdered guards, who had been thrown atop the carriage for the duration of the trip, were taken in by the old man. He told my uncle and the surviving guards that he and his nephew would contact their families and pay for their funerals out of thanks.

The old man thanked the hired hands told everyone involved that as a bonus they could keep the horse and guns they were given at the start of the journey, on top of their promised pay. My uncle was the last one to get his money. The carriage driver handed out everyone's due while the old man helped his nephew into the manor under the curtain of the approaching night.

As my uncle took his pay from the driver, he glanced over at the young aristocrat being helped out of the carriage and froze in fear. I heard my uncle recall that he'd never seen such a pale, withered young man before. He was an albino and according to what was passed down, the wealthy youth had eerily yellowish long nails, sharp ears, and eyes as black as those of a shark.

My uncle supposedly used to say he could have looked past all that if it wasn't for the bloodstains he'd quickly spotted around the young man's mouth. My uncle only saw the young man for a few moments, before the carriage driver purposely stepped in front of him, obscuring his view, and thanking my uncle for his protection.

My uncle nodded, and left, never to hear from or about the mysterious aristocratic youth ever again. Now I know what you're thinking, and believe me, I'm thinking it too. But you have to understand, it was a simpler time back then. The age of reason had sunk its claws into everyone, and I doubt my uncle would have jeopardized such a great payday all on the vague suspicion that the man who hired him was protecting a vampire.

Jinja

I'm not sure how to describe it. I was a nurse in a run-down hospital on the edge of Tokyo. Years prior the hospital had been an orphanage and after a fire burned it down, killing everyone inside, it was built back up. I had gotten hired during my last year of college and spent two years there, aiding the doctors who seemed to care little for the patients.

It was an easy enough job as no one ever came in with anything seriously wrong with them. On the second floor, at the end of a dead-end hallway, there was this little stone pond and fountain shrine that had been built in honor of the children who had died when the orphanage burned down.

There was always this little old lady, Miyuko, who came in for daily checkups and always warned us about disturbing the standing stones of the children's shrine on the second floor. She used to tell the doctors that if anything happened to the shrine a great misfortune would befall all those within the hospital.

The doctors shrugged off Miyuko's warnings and the nurses turned it into an urban legend that managed to spread across Tokyo. It was all fun and games until one night, following a short power outage and a light rainstorm, some new hires decided to play basketball up and down the second-floor hallway.

Inevitably one of them bounced the ball far enough to where it hit the shrine and the six standing stones, each of which bore the names of ten of the deceased orphans from the fire. Four of the stones fell back into the water, while the fifth remained standing. Unfortunately, the stone to the far right was pushed forward upon the basketball's escape from the pond which caused it to shatter onto the floor.

Believe me when I tell you everyone throughout the hospital heard that stone shatter. It was like an unnatural echo that rung through every corridor of that building. Needless to say, I came running to assess the damage, but it was too late. The lights dimmed as every clock throughout the hospital spun out of control.

In an instant, every mirror shattered and every exit slammed shut and locked. Those of us who had been left alone to lock up for the night were trapped inside as a black mist covered the exterior of the hospital, making it impossible to tell what was going on outside. The phones and computers went dead as black candles began popping up in places where they hadn't been before.

I fixed the shrine best I could and mended the broken standing stone with liquid cement from the storage closet. When I returned the new hires that had disturbed the shrine were gone. Two of the other nurses and myself later found them dead, sprawled out on beds lined up in one of the rooms, and filled with syringes and scalpels.

As the night progress, a few more of the staff members turned up dead. One had had his limbs sawed off and was writhing around on the table in the operating room, while another had had her mouth sewn shut and her eyes pulled out. It was after coming across the last one that we began to see the children.

They wore white gowns, had blue, transparent skin, and black eyes with red pupils. The later it got the more they began to appear and the clearer we were able to see them. We ran all night, watching the spirits of the dead children chase down, drag away, and murder each person within the hospital one by one.

The only reason I survived, I suppose, was because I didn't stop running. Not until it was morning and the black mist enveloping the hospital faded away. When it was all over the black candles vanished as the lights went back to normal. I visited the upstairs shrine to see that the standing stone that had broken was mended with no signs of damage whatsoever.

As I inspected the shrine I happened upon a picture next to some flowers I had never noticed before behind the stones. Picking it up, I noticed the photograph was of all the children from the old orphanage standing around their caretaker. An old woman who suspiciously looked all too similar to the elderly Miss Miyuko.

My heart fell into my stomach as I ran for the door, desiring nothing more than to leave that hospital and never come back. As I broke past the front doors I felt the morning sunshine upon my face. I fell to my knees, gasping for breath, and was met with a line of officers who slowly began to close in on me.

I was hauled off and detained as the hospital was searched and the victims were tallied. In the end, I was blamed for the murder of eight nurses, one doctor, two technicians, and six patients. Not even the hospital's surveillance, which would have proven my innocence, could be recovered. I was deemed insane, even after making up a cover story, knowing no one would believe my tale about the ghost children, and asked by the local press if I had anything to say before I was locked up for life.

I looked into their cameras and begged everyone to never disturb the second story children's shrine of the Masayuki Hospital in Tokyo, Japan.

The Blaque Masque

I remember hearing once about this foul-tempered aristocrat who was so obsessed with his appearance that he slept with a large mirror adjacent to his bed. Every night it was said that he would sit alone in the dark and stare at his own reflection before falling asleep. The long and the short of it was that one night the aristocrat's reflection leaped out of the mirror and killed him before taking the man's place in the real world.

The only reason his friends and loved ones caught on was due to the aristocrat's lack of a reflection in every mirror he stood before. Eventually, the man went missing after proving in some small way that something as innocent as our reflections may be eviler than we suspect. It is for this reason that I never sleep in a dark room containing a mirror larger than the size of my hand.

That tale sure did unsettle me, but it's nothing compared to the Tale of the Mask of Count Le Blaque. Oh, you've never heard it? Well, in that case--pull up an antique armchair, sit before a roaring Victorian fire, and let me pour you some English brandy as we drive right into the heart of this thing! It went down like this, see.

Supposedly there once lived a French Count by the name of Le Blaque who was said by all to have been as handsome as he was strange. He was an odd soul with a fascination for the macabre and the bizarre who had built up a reputation as a collector of unnatural relics and supposedly supernatural artifacts.

In the summer of 1818, Le Blaque somehow obtained a somber-looking paper mache mask which he said possessed the horrifying ability to take its wearer's life if they had it on past midnight. Now the mask was sleek, black, and looked like something you'd wear at a masquerade ball. Le Blaque enjoyed flaunting his find, eventually inviting one of his longtime friends, Lord Dauphine, over for dinner and a test run of the mark's supposed curse.

Dauphine arrived at the manor by carriage at eight and brought with him a great sense of curiosity concerning Le Blaque's belief in his collection of oddities. After dinner, and the consumption of much vintage wine, Le Blaque and Dauphine settled into the drawing room where the Count donned the mask and planned to wait for the arrival of midnight alongside his inquisitive guest.

As the two awaited the dawning of the deathly hour, Le Blaque spoke of how he planned to leave his fortune to Dauphine if the mask did take his life by midnight. He even went so far as to present his friend with the proper paperwork to confirm his promise. Dauphine, half touched by the Count's display of spontaneous charity, did the same.

After hastily filling out pre-notarized wills and forms which named Le Blaque as the sole benefactor of Dauphine's fortune, the air of trust and respect in the room felt leveled. That all changed, of course, the moment midnight came around. At the stroke of ten minutes short of the final hour, it was Dauphine who fell to the floor, weak and barely able to speak.

Le Blaque loomed over him, smiling through a face of malevolent delight. The Count confessed that the process of the cursed mask had already begun, that, in reality, it was those who were in the presence of the mask's wearer that died following the stroke of midnight. When confronted about his nefarious plan, Le Blaque confessed that his obsession with collecting rare and unnatural objects had caused him to go nearly broke.

As a way of replenishing his fortune, the Count boasted about how he had—for the better part of the last year—been killing aristocrats via the curse of the black mask after convincing them in some way to sign their fortunes over to him in the event of their improbable deaths. Having heard the method in which Le Blaque planned on obtaining newfound wealth.

Dauphine laughed and sprang to his feet a mere three minutes before midnight. Le Blaque, speechless and frozen in shock, watched as Dauphine pulled a duplicate black mask out from under his jacket. As the Count, stricken with astonishment, fell into his armchair, Dauphine revealed that he suspected foul play.

He revealed knowledge that Le Blaque had let his guard slip and that Dauphine had swapped out the Count's deadly mask with a fake after receiving his dinner invitation. You see, Dauphine was no slouch. Hell, he was a part-time sleuth, and over the course of the last year, he had secretly connected the deaths of multiple aristocrats back to Le Blaque.

Dauphine knew the Count's new mask was to blame, but he couldn't tell why. That's why he had befriended Le Blaque, that's why Dauphine accepted his invitation, and that's how the Count was finally outsmarted. With two seconds to go, Dauphine put on the real mask as the clock struck midnight. Just as predicted, Le Blaque died, a grimace of fury fixed upon his face.

No one's really sure about what happened to Dauphine after that. I mean, he obviously inherited Le Blaque's entire fortune, as well as all of his supernatural relics. But like most stories from the past, there's no telling whether this one is true or not. Like the mean old aristocrat and his murderous reflection, this story will probably wind up forgotten just like the rest of those old European tales of weird suspense and pulp horror.

Each of them, be it about a cursed ring, a haunted wardrobe, or a demonic painting, always puts me on edge. The only difference with this one is that the object of the story's narrative didn't make me fear masks like I would have feared rings, wardrobes, and paintings. On the contrary, it made me fear out-of-the-blue dinner invitations from people I barely know.

You never know who is gunning for you these days or in what manner, be it supernatural or otherwise, they plan to take you out.

Horror at Highgate

My name is Special Agent Icarus Crane of the international intelligence agency known as Blue Rose. This is my report. I'm laying here having just neutralized what amounts to a human with the features of a plant. That said, he has the torso of a man, but the head of a rose made up of pulsing pink flesh.

His arms are skin and muscles, but his hands extended into long thorn-covered whip-like vines that are still twitching even now. Wilted leaves and odd yellow spines protrude from his back while horn-like branches extend out from where his shoulder bones and elbows should be. When I first came across him he was shrieking and flailing and running straight at me.

I doubt he understood a single command I shouted at him. I knew he couldn't understand. The first thing he did was turn his back to me. When I told him to turn around boney spikes, not unlike those of a porcupine, came flying at me from beneath the foliage masking his upper back. They struck me in the left arm, burying themselves deep as if they had been fired from a crossbow.

I wasn't given much time to think about my reaction after that. The first bullet I put into him went clean through his right shoulder. It didn't deter him at all. After being struck with one of his vine-like appendages I attempted to disable the assailant by shooting him twice in each leg. This failed as he still scrabbled to reach me after hitting the floor.

Realizing I had no other choice I shot the target six times in the torso. After this failed to stop him I fired three more rounds into his head which finally put him down. After putting two more bullets in him for good measure I took a moment to address the wounds I had received during the altercation. He was definitely the biggest out of all the mutant hybrids I had encountered today.

I was deployed to the suburb of Highgate in northern London after headquarters received multiple reports of strange individuals attacking locals in and around the town's cemetery. Before I could even get past the gates I was bombarded by snarling individuals with green skin and yellow eyes leaking acidic puss.

Once I finally made my way into the cemetery I encountered open graves with mutated plants and reanimated corpses running amok. I naturalized as many as I could before rescuing four civilians and finally finding cover near an old chapel. After calling for backup and checking in with Agent Green, who had arrived on site shortly after me, I proceeded toward the center of the cemetery where I deduced the source of the incident had originated.

Green broke off to search for more civilians and to contact me once backup arrived. I must have gunned down close to thirty plant-like humanoids before stumbling upon a rather peculiar mausoleum. It didn't take long for me to locate a terribly hidden and slightly ajar door at the rear of the chamber.

A door that led to a series of recently renovated catacombs that must have been centuries old and ran beneath the entirety of Highgate Cemetery. After radioing my findings into Green and the other agents who had recently arrived on scene, I proceeded into the underground. There I discovered similar hybrids to the ones I had encountered in the graveyard, but with far more plant-like features.

Their heads were petals and their arms were stiff, bloody branches that lunged their bodies forward every time they attempted to swing them. They were easy enough to get past before moving into more occupied quarters. It wasn't long before I came across the eviscerated body of the man who had been responsible for all this carnage.

It was none other than the celebrated geneticist and biochemist, Doctor Quentin Price. A studious man of misled ambition and no restraint, as his peers would say. Shortly after finding him with his chest ripped open I accidentally awoke the slumbering behemoth I mentioned prior. According to what notes I was able to analyze during my short jaunt through the lab, the giant I had gunned down was called “Bud” and happened to be the demented Price’s crowning achievement, whatever the hell that means.

I collected what data I could and in a few minutes I’ll be rendezvousing with Agents Green, Crystal, Taylor, and Harris. After catching a chopper out of here, Blue Rose’s collateral team will fly in and take care of the rest. Just like they always do. Whatever Price was attempting to accomplish by reanimating and mutating the bodies of the dead I will never know.

All I can say for sure is that Blue Rose burned the twisted fool's research along with his subterranean lab in the hope that this sort of thing will never happen again.

The Erotic Adventurer

Inspector Dauphine, representative of some high-ranking establishment of authority, held the relic of a distant world in the gloved palm of his right hand. It was a brass sphere covered in cubic runes and humming something in Gregorian. He glanced it over once or twice, coming to the realization that the destruction of the sphere meant the destruction of a planet.

That planet being the one he stood upon whose name was Pheth, or Theph, or something like that. It was all quite Egyptian. Dauphine had been walking for what felt like two consecutive years through an orange desert under purple skies. The stars at night were unlike those of his home world, as they seemed to portray traits distinguishing them as living beings, rather than clusters of exploding gas.

There was something mystical about Pheth, or Theph, or whatever it was called. Dauphine, who had visited a thousand worlds before, stood in awe at the mythical simplicity of the realm. The pyramids off in the distance were transparent amethyst with golden peaks and intricate interiors. Somehow Dauphine could tell.

He had faded out of an age of modern chaos and into the tomb of a dead god who had boasted the body of a man and the head of a crow. It was in this tomb, lined with piles of frankincense and myrrh, that Dauphine discovered the brass sphere upon a misty slab of polished azure crystal. It didn't take long for Dauphine to pocket the relic and split, lending credence to the rarely discussed fact that he had once been a prolific treasure hunter.

What felt like a two-year hike across the desert might have actually lasted two days. Then again, Dauphine knew that time was relative. After taking ownership of the sphere, he vowed to keep it safe for the sake of Pheth, or Theph, or... yeah. Realistically there were two reasons Dauphine had appropriated the brass relic.

The less-than-noble reason was due to the fact that Dauphine was a collector of rare and ancient objects. The other reason was that Dauphine knew the sphere was better off in his back pocket than in some hole in the ground. He reasoned that tombs were raided all the time and that, if he hadn't stumbled upon it, the fragile sphere might have fallen into more nefarious hands.

That's usually how Dauphine justified his actions. Especially those involving the theft of priceless objects from across distant dimensions. That didn't mean Dauphine was wrong. Because of his low-grade kleptomania, Pheth, or Theph, or so on would never fall into darkness. With its deities dead and its population extinct, the infinite plane of sands, skies, and scattered ruins would sit preserved in the back pocket of Dauphine's favorite scarlet jacket.

It was a long frock coat with golden buttons and a lapel large enough to host two platinum crests. Before leaving, Dauphine was obviously confronted by the enraged ghosts of the plane for taking the sphere. They appeared in the form of ghastly wraiths and shrieking shades that threatened to haunt Dauphine until the end of his days.

Unfazed by the encounter, Dauphine scoffed and tapped the base of his black and gold cane twice against the dusty ground. In the blink of an eye, he was in another place in time, free from the clutches of a lost world's ravenous revenants. In the palm of his hand, Dauphine held the dead world as he had held so many others.

Secretly he longed for their revival and dreamed of days that would never be.

Oi vey! You Old Mensch

My buddy Mannis Shimmel, whose full name was Mannis Zaydel Ancel Faivish Shimmel, was a Yiddish poet who sometimes went by the epithet Mzafs. His five-part moniker, which literally translated to "God is with us, grandfather. Fortunate, bright, and listening," had always been the bane of my friend's existence.

"Shimmel this, Shimmel that, Shimmel had a heart attack," kids would say to him in the schoolyard. "Zaydel Ancel found a pencil, Zaydel Ancel had an asshole," they'd chant over and over again. They'd ask him, "What is your Mannis Operandi?" and other repetitive shit like that.

Mzafs ignored them best he could and kept to himself for most of his youth. As he grew, my friend read countless dirty limericks and studied the art of the pun to pass the time. Wordplay became his best friend as his uncle, Yohanan Shimon Judah Rabban, who kinda looked like the musician Allan Sherman, trained his nephew in the sacred craft of Hebrew humor.

In his life, Mzafs had published three successful poetry collections. The first of these was "The Schlepping Kvetch", followed by "The Shande's Schtick", and finally "The Klutz with No Chutzpah" which rounded off what became my friend's legendary trilogy. Each one sold better than the last, and for a while Mzafs found true happiness. That was until his abduction.

I believe he was sixty when it happened. If you know anything about the Ascended Masters and the lore surrounding Atlantis, then you'd know that time-traveling Hebrews are just one of a series of hilarious facets fixed firmly into the mythology surrounding the origins of Lemuria. Mzafs was one such person who believed these tales and swore that saucer-piloting Yiddish folk from the future were attempting to abduct him for some unknown purpose.

He told this to me in confidence over the course of two years before his disappearance. At the time it seemed unbelievable, but now I'm not so sure anymore. I suppose it could have been true that fans of Mzafs' work could have been ballsy enough to travel back in time to keep his influence alive millions of years from now.

I'm not saying Mzafs' work has the ability to bring world peace or anything like that, but his poems were pretty funny. I suppose in their own small way whoever took my friend knows what they're doing. As long as they bring him back to us one day, I'm sure Mzafs won't mind either. As long as they have at least one kosher deli and allow him to rest on Shabbos.

FIN

www.ingramcontent.com/pod-product-compliance
Lightning Source LLC
LaVergne TN
LVHW010510160826
845677LV00012B/2770

* 9 7 9 8 3 6 4 7 0 7 8 8 8 *